MONEY MATTERS

School Fundraisers

Problem Solving with Ratios

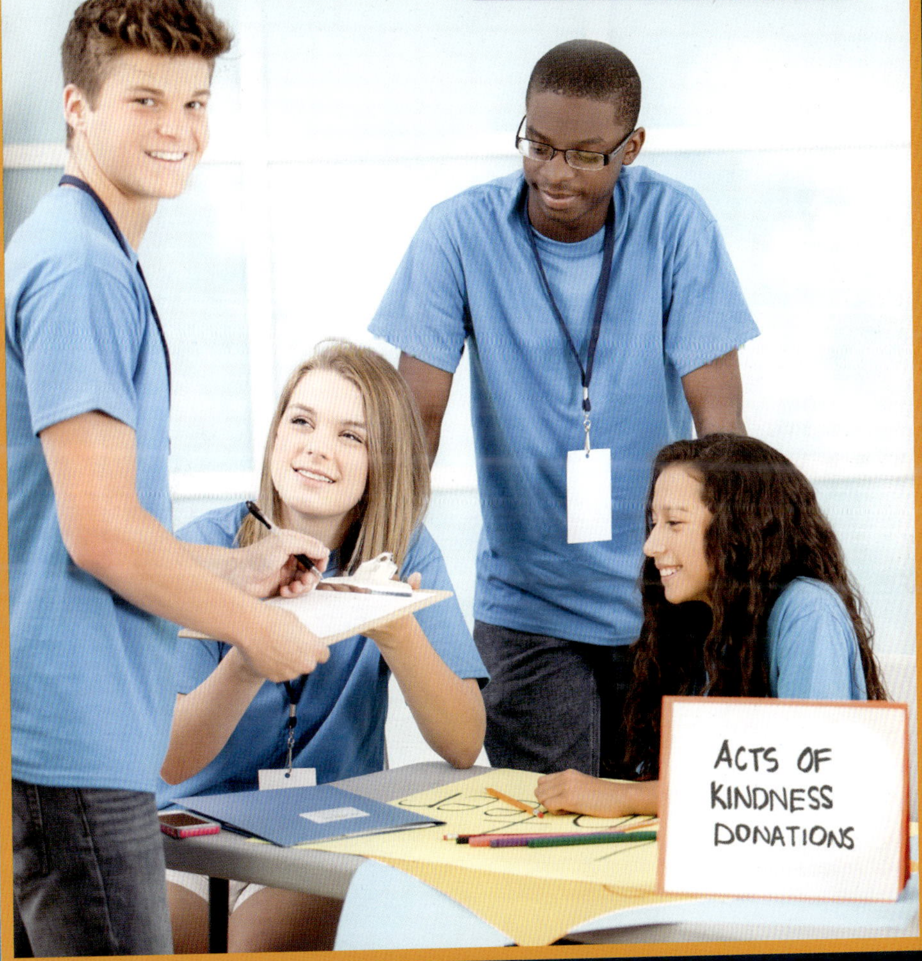

Georgia Beth

Contributing Author

Alison S. Marzocchi, Ph.D.

Consultant

Colleen Pollitt, M.A.Ed.
Math Support Teacher
Howard County Public Schools

Publishing Credits

Rachelle Cracchiolo, M.S.Ed., *Publisher*
Conni Medina, M.A.Ed., *Editor in Chief*
Dona Herweck Rice, *Series Developer*
Emily R. Smith, M.A.Ed., *Series Developer*
Diana Kenney, M.A.Ed., NBCT, *Content Director*
Stacy Monsman, M.A., *Editor*
Michelle Jovin, M.A., *Associate Editor*
Fabiola Sepulveda, *Graphic Designer*

Image Credits: All images from Shutterstock and/or iStock.

Library of Congress Cataloging-in-Publication Data

Names: Beth, Georgia, author. | Marzocchi, Alison (Alison S.), author.
Title: Money matters : school fundraisers : problem solving with ratios / Georgia Beth ; contributing author, Alison S. Marzocchi.
Description: Huntington Beach, CA : Teacher Created Materials, [2019] | Audience: Grade 4 to 6 | Includes index. |
Identifiers: LCCN 2018047788 (print) | LCCN 2018057685 (ebook) | ISBN 9781425855246 (eBook) | ISBN 9781425858803 | ISBN 9781425858803¬q(pbk.)
Subjects: LCSH: Ratio and proportion--Study and teaching (Elementary)--Juvenile literature. | Problem solving--Juvenile literature. | Word problems (Mathematics)--Juvenile literature. | Educational fund raising--Miscellanea--Juvenile literature.
Classification: LCC QA117 (ebook) | LCC QA117 .B48 2019 (print) | DDC 372.7/1--dc23
LC record available at https://lccn.loc.gov/2018047788

Teacher Created Materials
5301 Oceanus Drive
Huntington Beach, CA 92649-1030
www.tcmpub.com

ISBN 978-1-4258-5880-3

Printed in Malaysia
Thumbprints.21254

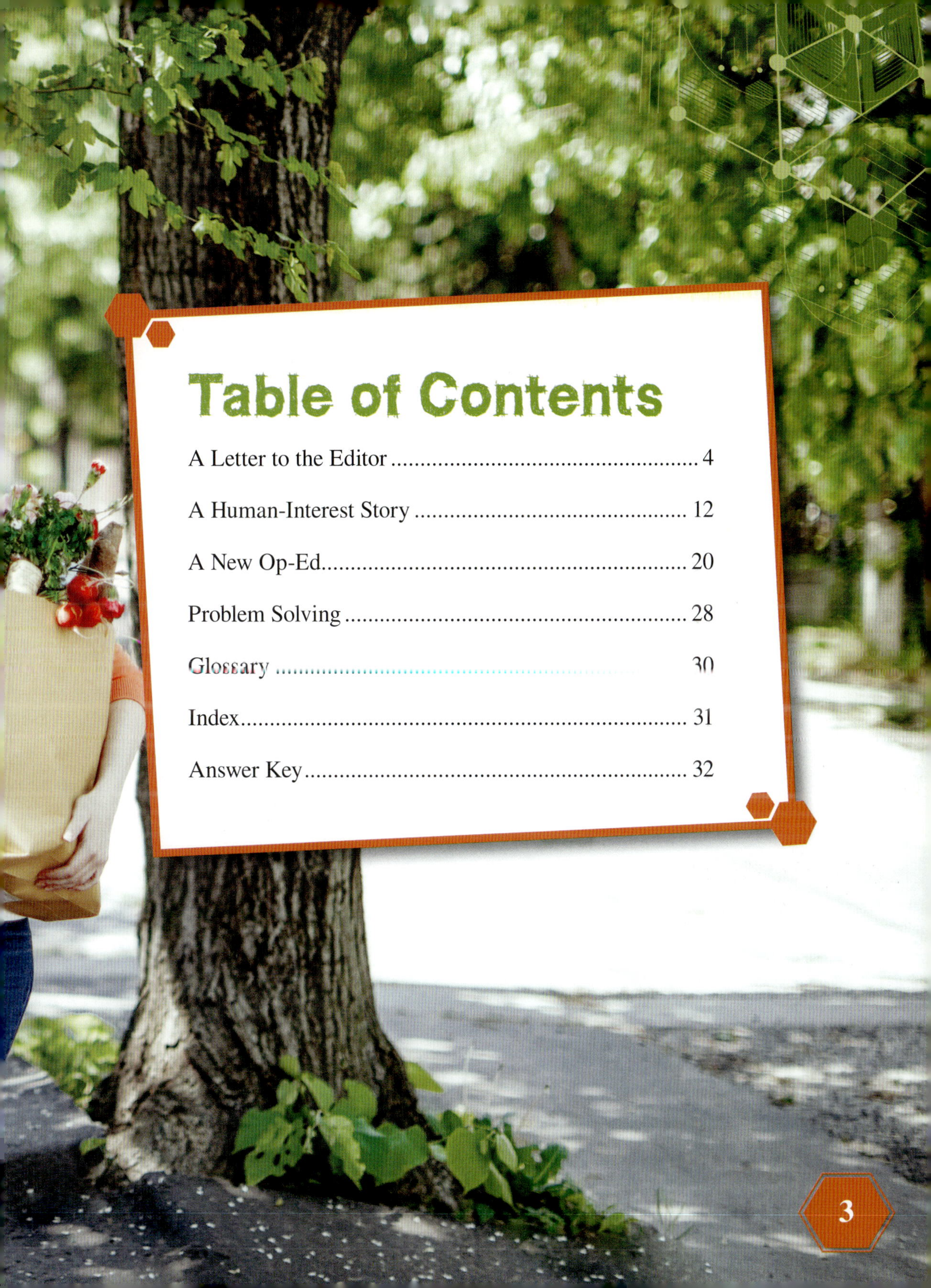

Table of Contents

A Letter to the Editor

The sign read "Student Body President," but it could have also said "The Guy Who Knows Everyone." Broderick peered out from a crack in the door. Getting to know people before they ever spoke a word helped him become friends with everyone, from the **valedictorian** to the custodian. His office was where he wrote his speeches and practiced his handshakes. The walls were covered with layers of old posters, trophies, and quickly scribbled jokes on sticky notes. A stack of newspapers was spread out on the desk.

"Quarterback Out for the Season!" "Librarian Bans Most Requested Books!" "Spring Break 2 Days Shorter This Year!"

"Seriously? Why don't they just print lightning bolts and a black cloud on the front page? This newspaper is **unmitigated** gloom and doom," Broderick said in frustration. He pushed a handful of papers at the student body **treasurer**.

"Dude, don't shoot the messenger! I'm just bringing you the latest. I don't write the headlines," Mateo said.

"Sorry. I'm really stressed. The principal said we have to cut $2,500 from the budget fast, so I'm reviewing every single extracurricular activity."

The Press

Douglass High S

e 101

uarterback ut for the Season!

ason Penn, Douglass High's star quarterback, sits the season out.

Story on page 2

Star Qu

Students study a robotic arm in a makerspace with their teacher.

Mateo gave Broderick a participation report from the **administration**. "What if we cut the debate team?"

Broderick scanned the numbers and objected, "Seven out of ten of the top Advanced Placement students and **International Baccalaureate** students are on the debate team."

"Good point. What about the 21st Century Makerspace?" Mateo offered.

"The principal told me 257 students visit every weekday, and 45 visit on weekends. Plus, it's pretty much the only activity keeping my brother in school," Broderick replied.

"Orchestra?"

"Band and orchestra are the biggest extracurriculars of all. Something like one out of four students participates," Broderick said. "And it's no better on the field. A lot of people like sports, and some of the teams make money for the school."

Mateo nodded his head in agreement.

"It looks like it's going to have to be the school newspaper," Broderick concluded. "Honestly, no one is even going to miss it. There are only about five people on the newspaper staff."

Mateo pulled out a notebook. "Let's get it done."

LET'S EXPLORE MATH

The report from administration also includes the numbers of males and females who participate in extracurricular activities. Broderick and Mateo analyze the data.

Extracurricular Activity	Number of Males	Number of Females
Debate team	7	8
Jazz band	22	18
Orchestra	26	22
Soccer	21	24

1. Broderick says, "This activity has a ratio of 11 males to 9 females." Which activity is he talking about?
2. Mateo asks Broderick, "What is the ratio of male soccer players to the total number of players?" How should Broderick respond?
3. Mateo says, "Look, these two activities have the same male to female ratio." Which two activities is he talking about?
4. Broderick says, "Orchestra has 4 more males and females than jazz band. So, orchestra and jazz band must have the same ratio of male to female students." Do you agree with him? Why or why not?

On Friday, when Evangeline got to school, she headed to the basement. Walking toward the newspaper office, her mind drifted to one of her favorite daydreams: choosing a pen name for next year's column. *Penelope? Or maybe I'll go totally* ***incognito*** *with Miguel.*

Her **reverie** was interrupted at the sight of an envelope. It was poking out from under the door to the school newspaper office.

To the Editor in Chief of Douglass High's The Press,

We regret to inform you that effective immediately, the student body council has elected to cut $2,500 in funds from the newspaper's budget. Please submit a new budget for approval or be subject to closure.

Douglass Forever!

Broderick Penn

Evangeline finds and reads the letter from Broderick.

Effective immediately??? Evangeline bristled. *This is exactly why I refused to vote for him.* She stomped to her desk and plugged her tablet into the **steampunk** typewriter. It had been a gift from her dad when she was named editor in chief. Evangeline fumed. There were more than a few things she might say to Broderick that he wouldn't forget. But she knew all he cared about was staying in office.

LET'S EXPLORE MATH

Yesterday, a reporter for *The Press* slid an envelope under the door. In the note, he claimed that he wrote fewer articles than past reporters. He wants to write more. Evangeline knows that reporters always share the work equally. She gathers some other data to compare reporter assignments.

Currently
5 reporters,
25 total articles
each month

When my dad was editor in chief
9 reporters,
45 total articles
each month

When my older brother wrote for *The Press*
6 reporters,
30 total articles
each month

1. How does the current ratio of articles per reporter compare to past years?
2. Imagine you are Evangeline. What would you tell the reporter who made the claim?

Instead, Evangeline pulled up the front page of the day's newspaper and bumped "Swim Team Battles the Flu" **below the fold**. Then, she wrote one of the most important pieces of her life.

She hoped with the paper being delivered before the weekend, she would have a big response.

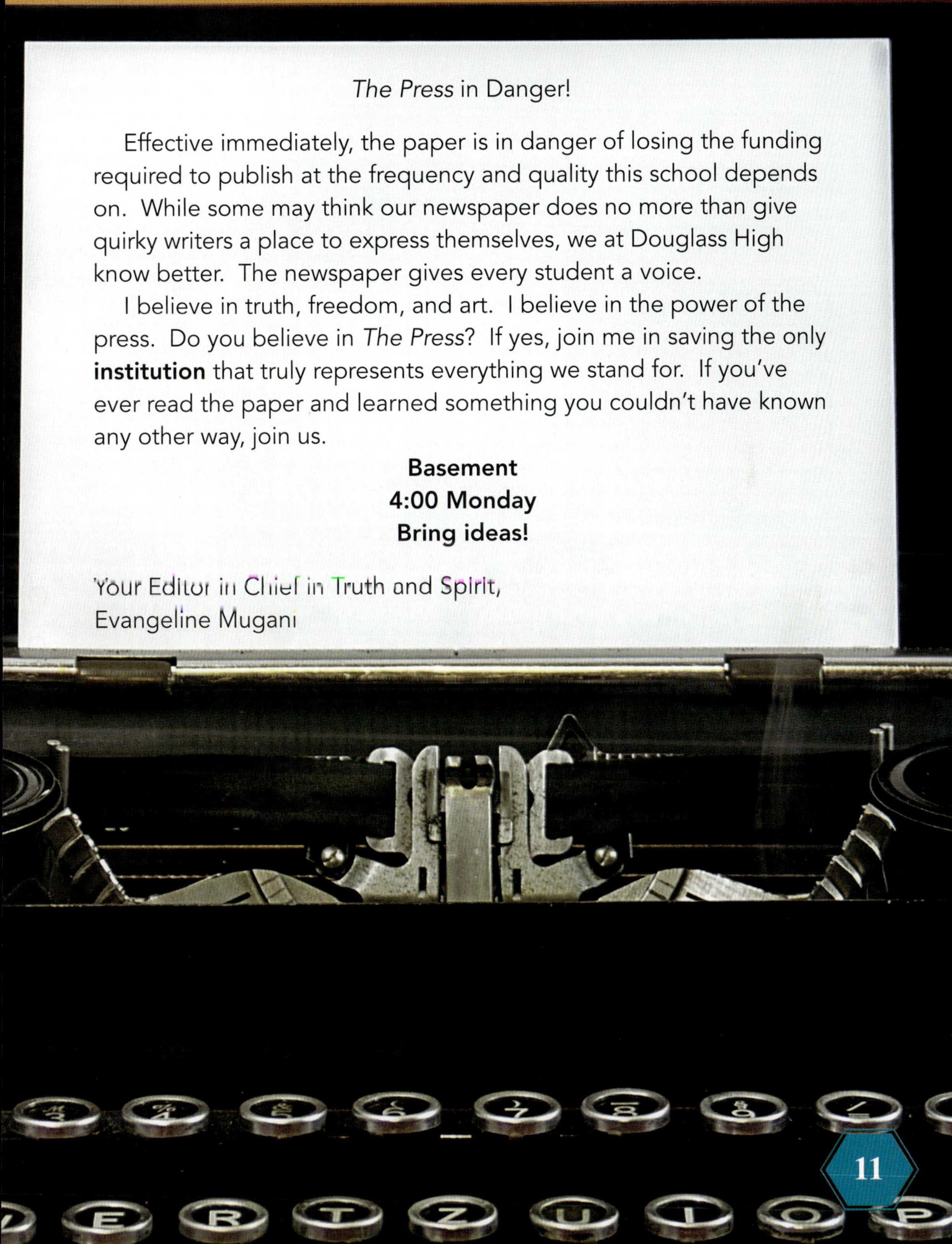

The Press in Danger!

Effective immediately, the paper is in danger of losing the funding required to publish at the frequency and quality this school depends on. While some may think our newspaper does no more than give quirky writers a place to express themselves, we at Douglass High know better. The newspaper gives every student a voice.

I believe in truth, freedom, and art. I believe in the power of the press. Do you believe in *The Press*? If yes, join me in saving the only **institution** that truly represents everything we stand for. If you've ever read the paper and learned something you couldn't have known any other way, join us.

Basement
4:00 Monday
Bring ideas!

Your Editor in Chief in Truth and Spirit,
Evangeline Mugani

A Human-Interest Story

When Evangeline arrived at school on Monday, her heart was heavy, but when she got to the basement at 4:00, she suddenly felt like she was in a dream and wide-awake at the same time. Over a hundred students were crammed into the chairs, slouched over desks, and hanging off cabinets. The floor was overflowing with backpacks, smelly shoes, and water bottles. Freshmen were hiding behind football players. The social media pros were taking selfies with the drama kids. It was a strange mix, but it was Douglass High in miniature form. These were *The Press*'s readers, and Evangeline intended to make them its heroes too.

Students take selfies before the meeting to save *The Press*.

After thanking the crowd for coming, she encouraged them to think of creative ideas to save the paper and handed out stacks of sticky notes. Whenever anyone had an idea, they stuck it to the chalkboard at the front of the room. Soon, the wall was covered in colorful notes. "Apply for a grant!" "Sell the paper off campus!" "Digitize!" "Charge $1.00 per copy!" "Do a fundraiser!"

LET'S EXPLORE MATH

One student suggests selling advertising space in the paper. Evangeline finds out that a neighboring high school's newspaper staff sells 5 advertisements for $60. She makes a rate table like this one to decide whether this is a good option.

Number of Advertisements	Cost
5	$60
10	$120
25	
	$900

1. What would 25 advertisements cost?
2. At this rate, how many advertisements does Evangeline need to sell to raise $900?
3. How many advertisements do you think *The Press* should sell? What would this number of advertisements cost?
4. Do you think selling advertisements is a good option to raise money for *The Press*? Why or why not?

Evangeline was excited until she saw Broderick and Mateo making their way past the **darkroom** and stepping over a pile of hockey gear on their way to the front of the room.

"What are you doing here?" Evangeline asked. "We're trying to solve problems, not create them."

"Hey, I come in peace, I promise. I didn't want to cut any extracurricular activities, but unfortunately the **statistics** don't lie," Broderick said.

"Nine out of ten students read this paper every month, and seven out of ten read it every week," Mateo replied.

"Seriously? How did I not have this data before?" Broderick asked **incredulously**.

"The administration just released the new set of statistics this morning," Mateo whispered.

"So *now* the statistics don't lie?" Evangeline interjected.

Ignoring her, Broderick eyed the wall of sticky notes and inquired, "What's that?" while he silently counted the number of students in the room.

"Those are all the ideas we've come up with so far," said Evangeline.

"Okay. I'll admit that it kind of sounds like we need to save *The Press*, but I don't know how yet," mused Broderick.

"Mind if we take a vote? You might as well make yourself useful while you're here," Evangeline said.

LET'S EXPLORE MATH

Mateo reports that 7 out of 10 students read *The Press* every week. There are 840 students at the school. How many of them read the paper every week?

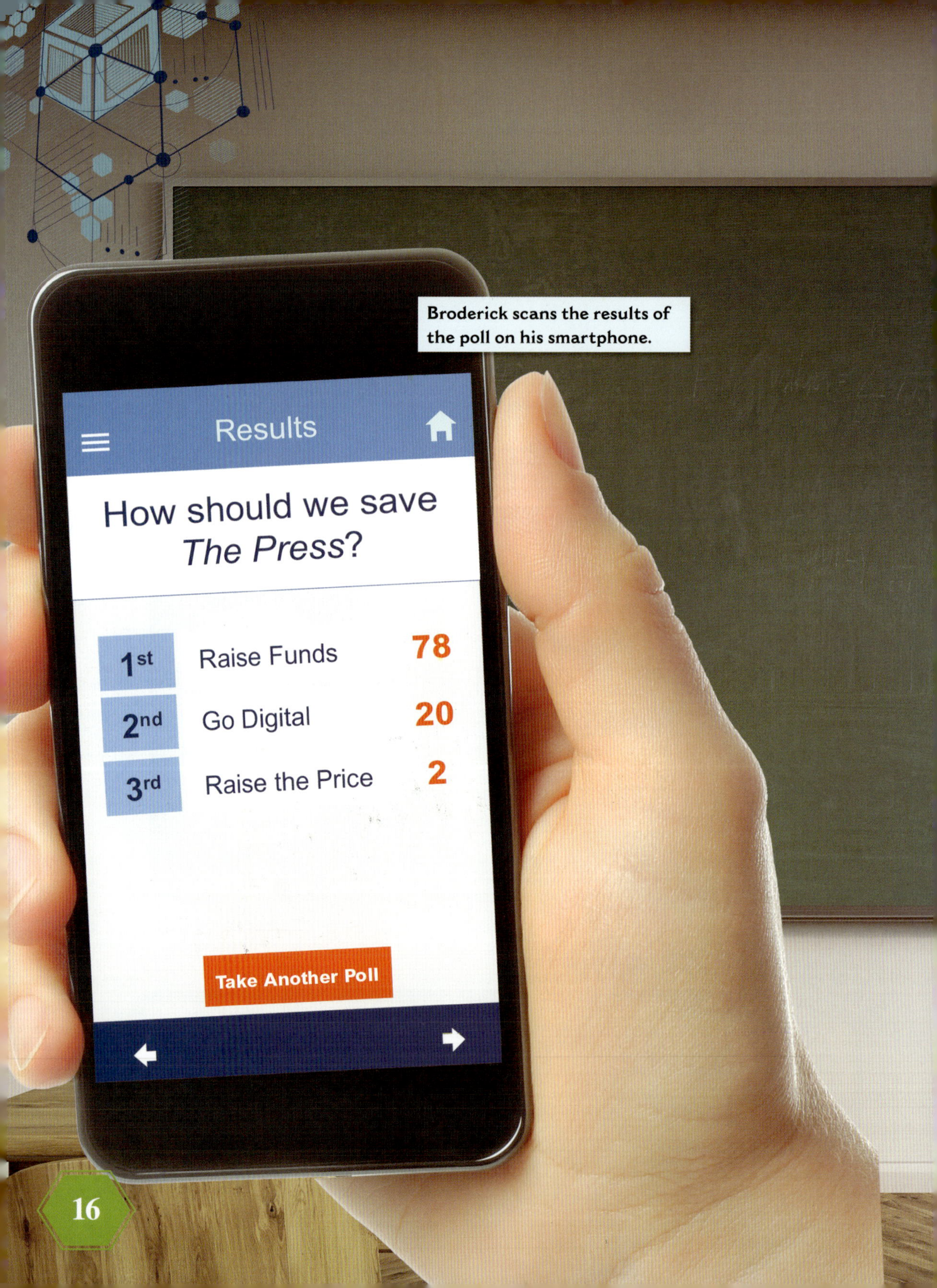

Broderick scans the results of the poll on his smartphone.

Broderick sorted the sticky notes into piles, scribbling the most popular ideas on the board for everyone to see, such as raising funds, raising the price, and going digital.

"Let's do a quick poll," Broderick began. "Give me a minute. I'll set up a question on a web app. You can see it on your smartphones or tablets." The students whipped out their devices and waited for Broderick to finish.

"OK, it's ready. Just respond right there in the app. I'll announce the winning suggestion," Broderick directed. Students swiped and typed as Broderick waited for the results to appear on his smartphone. They looked at him expectantly as he studied his screen. "Fundraising it is," Broderick finally announced without any real enthusiasm.

"Why do you sound so opposed to the idea? We could totally sell magazine subscriptions!" Evangeline suggested. "Journalism supporting journalism! That's got to get people excited to support *The Press*, right?"

Broderick winced. "Sure, but in my experience, fundraising tends to be more trouble than it's worth."

"What do you mean?" Evangeline asked.

"Bake sales are just school-sponsored sugar sales. Selling anything is a major undertaking, and there's no way I'm organizing a talent show. Marathons are out. They're super time-consuming and stressful. I want to help. I need to help. It's clear that a core **constituency** cares about *The Press*. But I don't think fundraising will rescue the paper."

The room was filled with students who were counting on Evangeline to keep the newspaper going, and she didn't want to disappoint them. A poster on the back wall caught her eye. It was a gift her mother gave her when she took over as editor in chief of *The Press*. The poster featured her mother's favorite quote: "Be the change you want to see in the world." Evangeline's fingers started flying midair as if she were tapping on the keys of an invisible typewriter, a quirky habit of hers whenever she was thinking of a new idea.

"What if…what if…" Evangeline turned to Broderick. "What if instead of a marathon, we hold a changeathon? What if we ask people to donate money in exchange for acts of kindness and courage, instead of running? No selling cookies, no spaghetti dinners, just kindness and courage."

Broderick smiled. "Instead of asking for help, we'll offer help?"

"Exactly! If people are kind enough to give us money, we can repay their kindness with kindness."

"Do you think we can raise enough money to save *The Press*?"

"There's only one way to find out," Evangeline said. "We've got a tremendous amount of work to do!"

BE THE
CHANGE
YOU
WANT TO
SEE
IN THE
WORLD

A New Op-Ed

The following week, there was a kickoff held to get the whole school involved. Faculty, staff, and students were invited to participate in the changeathon.

Mateo managed the site where students could track acts of kindness and get inspired by others. **Templates** let them email friends and family, asking for donations. The help-wanted page was filled with ways for students to get involved. People who liked getting to know new people could sit with new students at lunch. It was an easy way to earn a $5 donation. Those who liked being outside could pick up trash in the park. They raised $1,500 from neighbors who were glad to see it cleaned up. A couple of *The Press* reporters volunteered to write letters to soldiers who were deployed overseas. A veteran donated $100 in appreciation. Art students painted a mural to brighten the cafeteria. Others sent in $5 when they saw their improved lunchroom.

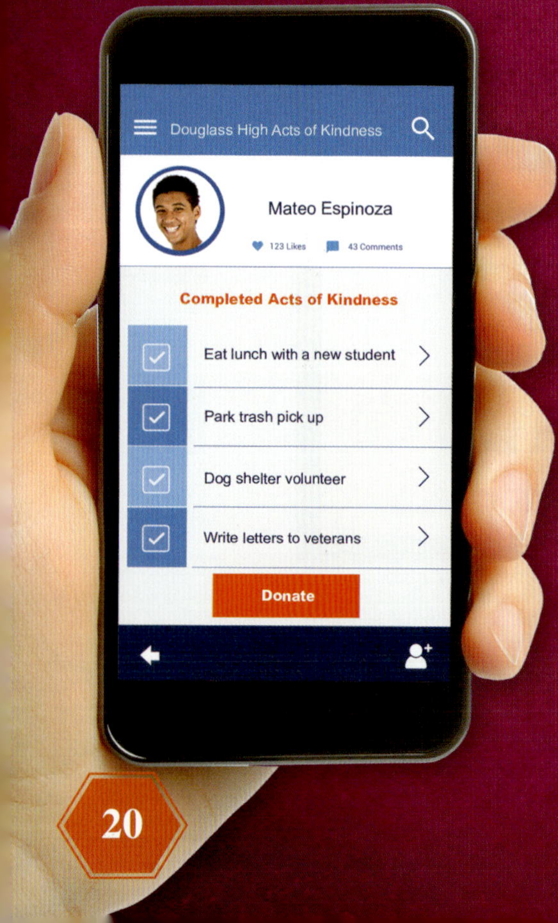

When someone finished performing an act of kindness, they logged in and added it to their profile. Once the act was registered on the site, someone could donate.

Students deliver groceries and clean up the park for their acts of kindness.

LET'S EXPLORE MATH

Several classmates each give a $5 donation for the new mural in the school lunchroom. Evangeline starts tracking the donations in a rate table.

Number of Donations	Total Money Raised
1	$5
2	$10
3	
4	
5	
6	
7	
8	
9	
10	

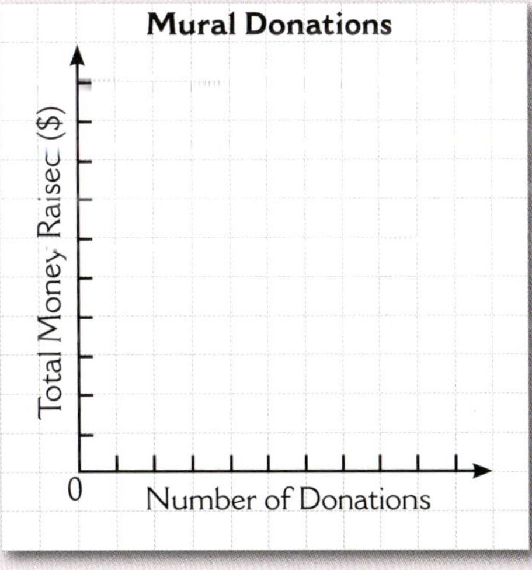

1. Use a rate table to track total money raised from 3 through 10 donations.
2. Evangeline wants to give Mateo a graph to show progress. Draw a graph like the one above. Label each axis with a scale. Plot each pair of values from the rate table.
3. When Mateo gets the graph, he plots (0, 0) on it. What does the point (0, 0) mean?

The different acts of kindness started to roll in, first 20, then 200, then 1,000! As they were performed, donations were tracked on the website. Most were small, just $5 or $10, but some were closer to $100. Evangeline wanted to keep the changeathon fresh in everyone's mind. So, she wrote about babysitting for a single mom and profiled the students who volunteered at the local food bank.

Evangeline tried to help someone every day. Soon, she had performed more acts of kindness than anyone. And who was right behind her? It wasn't a name she expected to see. But there it was—Broderick Penn, and he had done more than shake hands. He had helped build a community garden and had painted the principal's office. He had even organized a clothes swap, so students could trade old clothes with each other.

Evangeline sent her reporters out to document everything. "Let's show readers what it really means to be part of the changes we want to see in the world."

The writers talked to neighbors who were delighted to have a block party for the first time. The workers at the animal shelter were grateful for help cleaning kennels and feeding the animals. The science teachers were glad to have help scrubbing their test tubes and **petri dishes** at the end of their long days.

Students organize donations at a food bank.

A volunteer feeds a dog at the animal shelter.

LET'S EXPLORE MATH

Sheila mows lawns for her changeathon act of kindness. In 3 hours, she mows 6 lawns.

1. Which ratio shows the unit rate of lawns per hour?
   - **A.** 3:6
   - **B.** 6:3
   - **C.** 1:2
   - **D.** 2:1
2. At this rate, how many lawns can Sheila mow in 8 hours?
3. At this rate, how long will it take her to mow 8 lawns?

But the real story wasn't the good that was done in the community; it was the experience the students had volunteering. "It felt good to be helpful," one student said. "I want to do this every year," another added. Evangeline smiled as she read the quotations. Her favorite was, "I love getting to help the newspaper. I feel like I'm getting more out of this than anyone else. It just feels good to know that I'm doing things that not only need to be done but should be done out of kindness. And I get to help make our school a better place."

Evangeline asked the newspaper's designers to create new graphics for *The Press*. They chose an uplifting font and designed sidebar treatments to celebrate students and teachers who were making the changeathon possible. At the end of the month, a brighter, more cheerful version of *The Press* was published. "Soccer Team Builds New Balcony for Drama Club" and "Community Garden Blooms with Wildflowers" were just some of the headlines. The paper was filled with happy news. And when Evangeline could report that $2,800 had been raised, she sent the latest edition with "*The Press* Is Saved!" headline to print. She grinned because she knew her parents were going to be proud. She was enormously proud of herself!

The Press's designers lay out the new issue.

DOUGLASS HIGH SCHOOL

Go Douglass Cougars!

THE PRESS

Volume 102

Changeathon STARS

Mrs. Reyes

Motivates her sophomore science class to volunteer by giving extra credit for each act of kindness performed during the school year.

Kevin Patel

Senior class president inspires senior class to participate in the changeathon!

Sign Up Now

Soccer Team Builds New Balcony for Drama Club

Jess Meyers leads her team in shop class.

On Tuesday, the soccer team hammered away to build the drama club a new balcony. "It's awesome that they wanted to help us!" says Nathaniel Gordon of the drama club. "It's been weird doing some scenes without a real balcony."

Props had been stacked on top of the balcony, which caused it to collapse about two weeks ago. "It was pretty old, so it's not too surprising. Thankfully, it was only props on the balcony and not any people!" says Mr. Celaya, the club advisor. The club has wanted to build a new balcony, but rehearsal schedules have made it difficult to find the time. Gordon said of the soccer team helping, "It shows what a great community our school has!"

Community Garden Blooms with Wildflowers

If you've walked through the quad lately, you may have noticed a small patch of bright flowers beginning to bloom. The garden of wildflowers, planted in an effort to help save bees, has begun to take shape and show its vibrant colors. While only some of the garden has begun to bloom, the rest of it is sure to catch your eye soon!

LET'S EXPLORE MATH

Students who planted wildflowers in the community garden had to buy 15 pounds of seed. Garden Grow nursery sold 3-pound bags of seed for $54. Perfect Plants nursery sold the same seed in 5-pound bags for $95. The students wanted the best buy for their money. Which nursery do you think the students chose? Why?

When Broderick got his copy of *The Press*, he grinned too. Above the fold, Evangeline had written one last profile. Despite being published in the paper, it felt like she had written a letter just for him.

He could have sat by and watched as the Douglass High community proved it was committed to saving The Press. *But instead, Broderick Penn performed more than 50 acts of service this month. He even read a copy of* The Press *for the Institute for the Blind. His work helped more people understand why we fought so hard to save this newspaper at a time when so many publications are going digital or cut entirely. Even writers know that actions speak louder than words—or handshakes. And it's clear that Broderick Penn is more than a friend to* The Press. *He is a friend to everyone at Douglass High. It's with pleasure that I officially* ***endorse*** *Broderick Penn for student body president in the coming election.*

They might never be best friends. But Broderick was pretty sure he would be getting one more vote in the next election. And saving *The Press* wasn't a bad way to start his campaign.

Broderick finds out that Evangeline has endorsed him for student body president.

Problem Solving

Students from a neighboring high school read about the changeathon in *The Press*. They decide to hold their own changeathon to raise money for new marching band uniforms. The student council met to brainstorm acts of kindness, estimate how long the acts take, and predict amounts of donations. Imagine you are a member of student council. Use the table on page 29, and answer the questions to help plan the changeathon.

1. Based on the predictions, what are the hourly rates for raking leaves and reading books?

2. What do you predict people will donate for playing cards at the senior center? Based on this prediction, what is the total donation for this act of kindness?

3. How many hours do you think it will take to help set up the carnival? Based on this prediction, what is the total donation?

4. Members of student council expect the same hourly rate for cleaning the playground and raking leaves. What is the total donation for this act of kindness?

5. Brainstorm your own idea for an act of kindness.

    a. Predict the number of hours and hourly rate. Use your predictions to calculate the total donation.

    b. You need to show the student council's treasurer that your idea is worthwhile. Make a rate table that shows earnings for 1–10 hours of work. Then, draw a graph and plot each pair of values from the rate table. What information can the treasurer learn by looking at the graph?

6. Including the donations from your act of kindness, what is the grand total student council hopes to raise with the changeathon?

Act of Kindness	Estimated Hours	Donation Per Hour	Total Donation
Rake leaves at the community garden	4		$32
Read books to a preschool class	3		$21
Play cards at the senior center	5		
Help set up the Town Day Carnival		$15	
Clean the playground	10		

Glossary

administration—a group of people who control the way a school, company, or other organization functions

below the fold—located on the bottom half of the front page of a newspaper

constituency—the people who have the right to vote for an elected official

darkroom—a room for making photographs, which is lit with a special type of red light

endorse—to show support or approval for

incognito—concealing one's identity

incredulously—unbelievingly

institution—a public organization or corporation

International Baccalaureate—a program that allows students to take advanced classes and develop areas of investigation

petri dishes—small glass or plastic dishes sometimes used in scientific experiments

reverie—daydream

statistics—data and other numerical information

steampunk—a style of fashion and design that combines historical elements with technological elements inspired by science fiction

templates—things that serve as models or forms

treasurer—a person who is in charge of the money that is taken in and paid out by a business or organization

unmitigated—not lessened or made less severe

valedictorian—the student with the highest grades in a graduating class

Index

Answer Key

Let's Explore Math

page 7

1. jazz band
2. 21:45, or 7:15
3. debate team and soccer
4. disagree; 26:22, or 13:11, is not equivalent to 22:18, or 11:9.

page 9

1. All ratios are equivalent to 5:1.
2. Answer should include that there have always been 5 articles per reporter.

page 13

1. $300
2. 75 advertisements
3. Answers should include total costs when each advertisement costs $12.
4. Answers should include opinions and reasoning.

page 15

588 students

page 21

1. $15; $20; $25; $30; $35; $40; $45; $50
2. 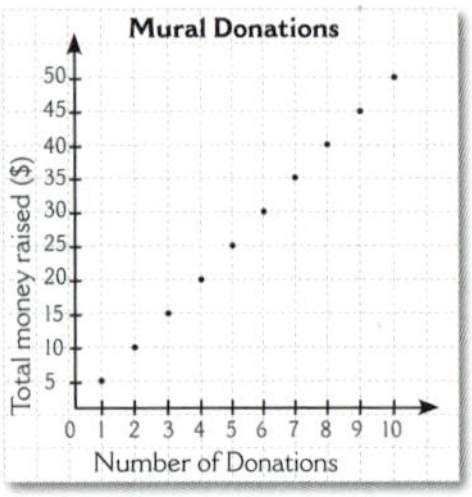

3. 0 donations raise $0.

page 23

1. D
2. 16 lawns
3. 4 hours

page 25

Garden Grow; Seed is 18 per pound, or $270 for 15 pounds. At Perfect Plants, seed is $19 per pound, or $285 for 15 pounds.

Problem Solving

1. $8; $7
2. Answers should include an hourly rate and total donation.
3. Answers should include estimated hours and total donation.
4. $80
5. **a.** Answers should include an act of kindness, estimated hours, hourly rate, and total donation.

   b. Rate tables and graphs should show donations for 10 hours of work. The treasurer can see how much money is earned per hour and total donations after each hour.
6. Answers should represent the sum of total donations.